The Big Book of
VAMPIRES

Editor: JESÚS ARAÚJO
Text: DENISE DESPEYROUX
Ilustrations: FERNANDO FALCONE
Design and page makeup: JORDI MARTÍNEZ
Proofing: JOAN and ALBERT VINYOLI
Research: J. TRÜFFEL

Original Spanish edition, El Gran Libro de los Vampiros,
published by Parramón Ediciones © 2011 Parramón Ediciones, S.A., Barcelona, Spain

The Big Book of Vampires
North American English edition published in Canada by Tundra Books
© 2012 Tundra Books, 75 Sherbourne Street, Toronto, Ontario M5A 2P9

Published in the United States by Tundra Books of Northern New York,
P.O. Box 1030, Plattsburgh, New York 12901

Library of Congress Control Number: 2011932738

Library and Archives Canada Cataloguing in Publication

Despeyroux, Denise
  The big book of vampires / by Denise Despeyroux ; illustrated by Fernando Falcone.

Translation of: El gran libro de los vampiros.
ISBN 978-1-77049-371-1

  1. Vampires--Literary collections. I. Falcone, Fernando, 1977- II. Title.

PZ5.D47Big 2013   j808.80375   C2011-904872-8

We acknowledge the financial support of the Government of Canada through the Book
Publishing Industry Development Program (BPIDP) and that of the Government of
Ontario through the Ontario Media Development Corporation's Ontario Book Initia-
tive. We further acknowledge the support of the Canada Council for the Arts and the
Ontario Arts Council for our publishing program.

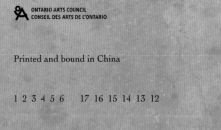

ONTARIO ARTS COUNCIL
CONSEIL DES ARTS DE L'ONTARIO

Printed and bound in China

1 2 3 4 5 6   17 16 15 14 13 12

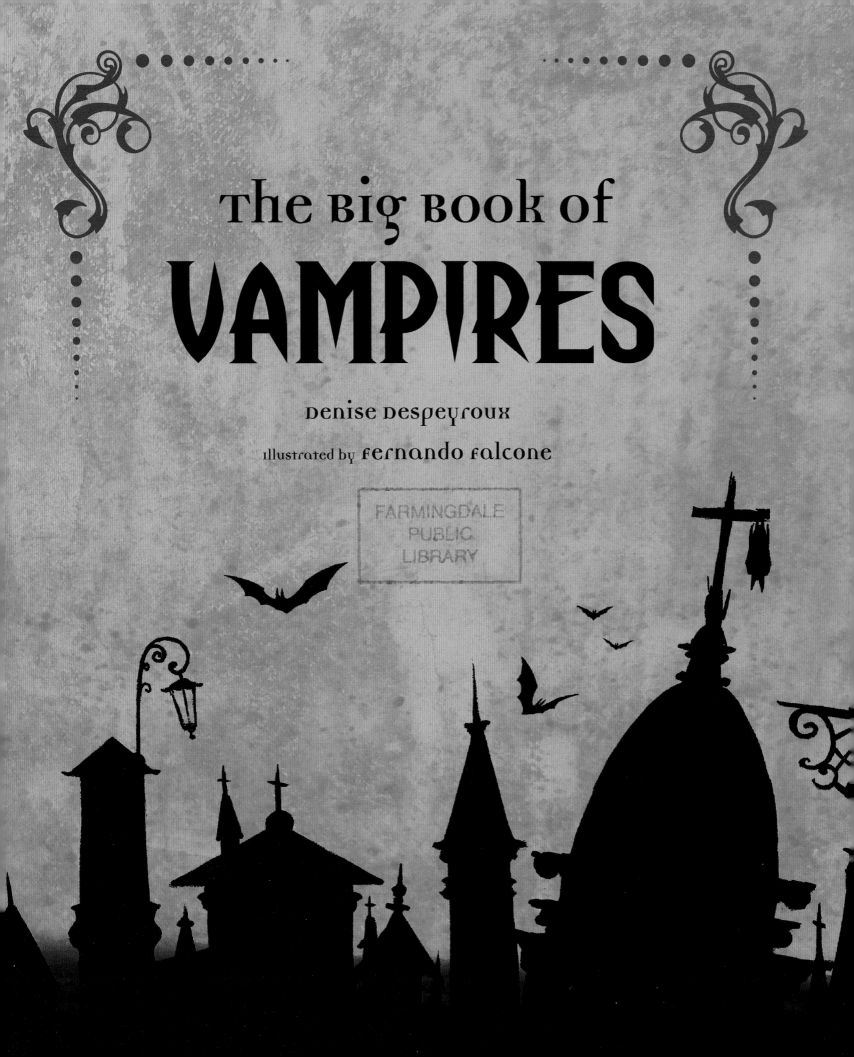

The BiG BOOK of VAMPIRES

DeNiSe DeSpeyroux

illustrated by Fernando Falcone

Contents

Introduction to the Vampire Stories

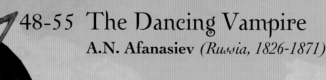

Contents

In this section of the book you will find nine adaptations of the most significant terror/vampire stories by the authors who brilliantly represent the literary genre of the nineteenth century.

Bram Stoker's **Dracula** quickly became the worldwide image of a cultured, refined, and bloodthirsty vampire. A man named Vlad Tepes was the living person who inspired the author.

Carmilla, by Sheridan Le Fanu, is a Gothic terror novel. It was as famous as *Dracula* – perhaps more so – though in the end, the image of male vampires won out over female vampires. *Carmilla* was also inspired by a real person, Elisabeth Bathory, who killed over six hundred young people because she liked bathing in their blood!

The Vampire, by John William Polidori, is a tale he penned after meeting with various writer friends in Geneva, Switzerland. Mary Shelley's Frankenstein also came out of that evening. What a productive night!

The Pale Lady, by Alexandre Dumas, is another famous vampire novel. It is written in the first person by the story's main character.

Vampire's Honor is a story from *The Thousand and One Nights*, a fascinating collection of Arabian tales from the medieval Middle East.

The Dancing Vampire, by A.N. Afanasiev, is a bloodthirsty story in the Russian literary tradition. The author collected and compiled hundreds of Russian tales.

The Family of the Vurdalak, by A.K. Tolstoy, must be one of the cruelest stories in this genre. The Vurdulak only chooses his victims from his own family members. He must have thought, the best blood is one's own.

Hoffmann's **Vampirism**, written in 1821, is thought to be the first tale whose main character, Countess Aurelia, is a member of the nobility – and a female vampire!

Thanathopia, by Rubén Darío, is the story of an estranged son who returns only to find he has a vampire stepmother. The author is the most outstanding representative of Modernism in Spanish literature and is known above all as a great poet.

Stories of Vampires

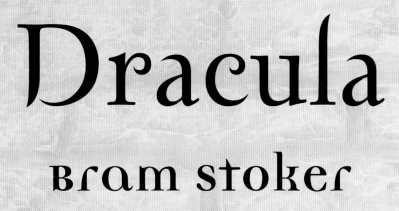

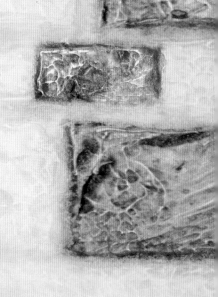

Dracula

Bram Stoker

(Ireland, 1847 – England, 1912)

THE ARRIVAL AT THE CASTLE

Young Jonathan Harker was a sensible man who was not prone to believe in popular superstitions. However, if he had to describe his journey to Count Dracula's castle in the Carpathian Mountains of Transylvania, the first words to spring to his mind would have been *spine-chilling* and *terrifying*. At each stop along the way, people crossed themselves and called upon God when they learned where he was going.

I'll sort out my business with this mysterious gentleman and return to my darling Mina as quickly as possible, he thought when he first spotted the dark, crumbling castle through the mist.

Young Harker was soon to marry a sweet and lovely young woman named Mina. This trip to Romania had delayed their wedding, but there was nothing to be done about it. The young lawyer had been sent to help the Count purchase a luxurious mansion in London. At least the wait would be worthwhile. The money earned from making the sale would be very useful to the newlyweds.

It was dark when the young man reached the castle, and Count Dracula came out to receive him in person. The Count was a tall, elderly, and extremely pale man. He offered his visitor supper, although he himself touched nothing. While Harker ate, he noticed the long, sharp fingernails of his host, and an unexpected shudder of fear ran down his spine.

The Journey to Europe

Try as he might, Harker was unable to finalize the sale with his host. Time passed, but Count Dracula was absent throughout each day, making it impossible to meet with him until nightfall. Even so, Dracula never dined with Harker. He just stared at his visitor while the young man ate. One evening, Harker cut himself with a knife, and when a small drop of blood appeared on his finger, the Count leapt toward him, letting out a strange groan. Startled, Harker instinctively reached for the cross he wore around his neck. To his surprise, the Count stopped and composed himself.

"Count Dracula," Harker said, gathering his courage, "I'm afraid I must close the deal tonight, as I have to return home to be with my fiancée, Mina."

The Count seemed interested to know more about Mina and asked Harker whether he had a portrait of her. The young man proudly showed him the one he always kept with him in a locket. He regretted it at once, when he saw the Count's expression.

"She has a beautiful throat," Dracula said. "Where are those papers? I will sign them and travel to London with you."

FLIGHT

That night, bathed in sweat, Jonathan Harker awoke from another dreadful nightmare. These night terrors had begun soon after his arrival at the castle, and they were making him weaker by the day. He rose and went over to the window. What he saw below froze the blood in his veins. Count Dracula was loading coffins onto a horse-drawn wagon. When he was finished, he ordered his coachman to leave for the port, where a ship to London was waiting. Then he climbed into one of the coffins and closed the lid. The coachman cracked his whip, and the horses sped away into the darkness.

Harker's heart almost stopped. He had put his love in terrible danger and would have to hurry if he was to save her. He tried to leave, but all the castle doors were locked, holding him prisoner! He dashed back up to his bedchamber and tied several sheets together. Then he fastened one end to the casement and climbed through the window and down. In his weakened state, the effort was too much for him. On reaching the ground, Harker fainted.

Some farm workers found him the next morning, and, seeing he was ill, took him to the hospital in Bucharest.

11

The Beast in London

In London, Mina was in a terrible state. She was pining for Jonathan and had begun having horrific dreams of her own. Her best friend, Lucy, had come to help, but was now suffering from some strange ailment. Lucy was sleepwalking at night. Each morning she was paler and weaker than the night before. Two blood-stained holes appeared on her neck and grew larger with each passing day.

Unable to understand what was happening, Mina consulted Professor Van Helsing, a specialist in rare diseases. The professor was very disturbed after his examination. He pointed to the two red holes on Lucy's neck, and what he said next was shocking.

"This young lady needs a blood transfusion, and she must be watched carefully every night. The marks on her neck have been caused by a vampire."

Mina's Decision

Van Helsing's incredible revelation left Mina profoundly upset. To make matters worse, Jonathan Harker had finally returned, but he, too, had terrible bite marks on his neck and was suffering from the same illness as Lucy.

"The only way to save them is to kill the beast that is doing this," Professor Van Helsing explained. "We will have to find the tomb where he sleeps by day and drive a stake through the center of his heart. And we must hurry. Otherwise, Jonathan and Lucy will become vampires too."

"But we don't know where his tomb is!" Mina cried. "There must be another way to kill him."

"There is, but it's very dangerous," the professor explained. "If a young maiden who is pure of heart can distract a vampire until dawn, he will surely die. That is because sunlight is fatal to vampires." Immediately, Mina decided to find the Count and detain him till sunrise. Dawn was already approaching. Without another thought, Mina hurried to the cemetery and sat on a grave-stone to await the prowling vampire.

VICTORY OVER EVIL

A shadow flitted among the trees.

"You're here, Mina," whispered Dracula. "I was going to come for you very soon. When your betrothed dies, I will take you to my castle. There you will reign alongside me for all eternity."

"I couldn't wait that long, my darling," Mina said, feigning love, even though she trembled in fear. "I wanted to become your wife this very night."

The Count fell into her trap and drew close to Mina. She held him with kisses and passionate words until the first rays of the sun peeked through the trees. The Count shuddered, a victim of violent spasms, but by then it was too late. The light, lethal to this creature of darkness, had seared him to the bone, leaving nothing more than a heap of ashes.

Mina fled home. There was Jonathan, waiting. He was restored to his true self and hugged his loved one. Lucy had also recovered completely and cried for joy in her friend's arms.

end

Carmilla

Sheridan Le Fanu

(Ireland, 1814-1873)

A Childhood Memory

My name is Laura, and I live with my father in an isolated castle in the mountains of Austria. Our nearest neighbors live in a village seven miles away. The ruins of a Baroque church are closer. Beside it, lie the tombs of an important aristocratic family, the Karnsteins.

My mother died when I was very young, and I grew up in the care of my loving father, a governess, and a nursemaid. One of my earliest memories has to do with a dreadful experience that wouldn't happen until much later, when I was nineteen years old. I'll tell you about it now, but be warned. This memory still holds the power to freeze the blood in one's veins.

When I was only about six, I awoke one night from a sound sleep with a strange feeling of unease. Alone in the dark, I began to cry. That's when I noticed a beautiful young girl at the foot of my bed. She drew close to comfort me, and I stopped crying. Then she climbed into bed and held me until I drifted peacefully off to sleep. But a short time later I awoke, screaming in terror and pain. It felt like two sharp needles had been driven into my chest. The young girl jumped up and seemed to hide under the bed.

Everyone in the household rushed in to assure me it was only a nightmare – everyone except my nursemaid. She told my father that someone had been in my room, but he ignored her. I remember that.

THE GENERAL'S LETTER

As I have said, the rest happened when I was nineteen. At that time, my father was expecting a visit from his friend, General Spielsdorf, who was going to stay a few weeks with us. He intended to bring his niece who was my age, and I was looking forward to her company. But one night my father asked me to go for a walk with him and explained the following:

"Laura, I have to give you some terrible news. The general won't be coming after all, as his beloved niece has died of some strange illness. The poor man is mad with grief. In his letter he raves about a monster to whom he gave shelter and says that his error cost the girl her life. He blames himself for her death.

Although I had not met Bertha, the general's niece, this news moved me deeply, and the letter, which I insisted on reading, made my hair stand up on end.

I was still holding the letter when the clatter of carriage wheels caught our attention. We looked up at the crest of a hill only to see a luxurious carriage plummeting toward us. One of the horses that drew it had bolted, and its panic had infected the others. The carriage struck a rock and overturned. Father and I ran forward to see if anyone was hurt.

AN UNEXPECTED GUEST

"I am the most unfortunate woman in the world," lamented a woman who managed to crawl out of the carriage. Meanwhile, the coachman and servants were trying to revive a young girl who had fainted. "What shall I do now?" the woman went on, appealing to my father. "I am traveling on a matter of life or death. Even one hour's delay could be crucial, but my daughter is in no condition to go on. Tell me, sir, how far is the nearest village? I have no choice but to take her there."

"Papa," I whispered in his ear. "Ask her to leave her daughter with us. I'll look after her, and she'll keep me company."

My father approached the lady and said solemnly, "You may leave the girl under my care and responsibility until your return, madam. It will be an honor to share our hospitality, I assure you."

I Saw You in a Dream

In all the commotion surrounding the accident, I could not properly see or speak to the girl that first night. But the next evening, I went to her chamber to meet her and offer my companionship. I approached her bed, but there I froze. Her face, beautiful and melancholy, was the exact same face I had seen as a child in my terrible nightmare.

"This is incredible," she told me. "Thirteen years ago I saw you in a dream, and I have never forgotten your face!"

Breathless, I told her she had been in my dream, too. Her name was Carmilla, and we became best friends. It was as if we had known each other forever. Still, Carmilla was unpredictable and acted strangely. She never received me during the day, and one night, with no warning at all, she said the strangest thing:

"Don't think me cruel if I obey the impulse that governs me. If your heart is wounded, mine bleeds too. I live for your warm blood and you, my dear, will die for mine."

The Countess Mircalla

One night, Father and I were unpacking some paintings, inherited from my mother, that we had sent to be framed. Among them was one that had Mircalla, Countess of Karnstein, written on the back. On turning the canvas over, we were both struck dumb for a moment.

"Why, it's a portrait of Carmilla!" I exclaimed at last.

"The likeness is astonishing," my father agreed.

"It's not as strange as it seems," Carmilla explained. "I am a distant descendant of the Karnsteins."

From that night on, I began to suffer from horrifying nightmares. Each one left me weaker. At times I awoke with sharp pains in my neck and chest and saw a woman beside me, dressed in black with long hair covering her face.

Now I lived in terror and became gravely ill with something no doctor could identify. My father sent for a foreign physician, an expert in rare diseases, who came to see me.

"You say that during your nightmares you feel two needles pricking your neck? Will you show me exactly where you feel the pain?"

I uncovered my neck and indicated an area just below my throat.

"You see these two little marks?" the doctor asked my father. "I have no doubt as to the cause of her illness."

THE RUINS OF KARNSTEIN

My father immediately ordered various maids to sleep in my bedchamber. They were not to leave me alone for a second. At first light he set out for the ruins of Karnstein. What happened there I learned from an official document some time later, for, as long as he lived, my father would never speak of that night.

Apparently he gathered several doctors and a priest. Together they searched for the grave of the Countess Mircalla. On opening it, they found our treacherous and most lovely guest. Carmilla … Mircalla … the same letters in different order … the same frightening creature.

Following ancient practice, they hammered a stake through the vampire's heart. According to the document, she shrieked a sharp death-cry before she lay dead.

I never saw Carmilla again, but a long time passed before I recovered from the horror of those events. You are the first to hear my story . . . . Sleep well tonight.

end

The Vampire

John William Polidori

(England, 1795-1821)

THE FRIENDSHIP BETWEEN LORD RUTHVEN AND YOUNG AUBREY

That winter, at the parties and soirées characteristic of London at that time, a mysterious nobleman appeared and drew much attention. To begin with, his physical bearing was striking. Although his face was unusually pale, and his strange gray eyes were somewhat unsettling, no one – male or female – could deny he was an extraordinarily attractive man.

Young Aubrey became fascinated by this aristocrat with the penetrating gaze. He was mysterious and solitary and seemed to pass hours wrapped up in his inner thoughts.

Aubrey's parents had died when he was a child, so he and his sister had been educated by tutors who were, unfortunately, more interested in cultivating imagination than good judgment. Soon Aubrey was so carried away by fantasy that Lord Ruthvan became a kind of fictional hero to him. Aubrey admired the man so much that he grew to trust him completely. One day, Aubrey spoke to Lord Ruthven of his intention to travel to Europe and was highly flattered when the mysterious gentleman offered to accompany him.

THE TRIP TO EUROPE

On traveling and sharing time with Lord Ruthven, Aubrey learned more about his companion's character and behavior. He noticed many details he had not seen before and disliked most of them. For example, his companion was accustomed to giving generously to beggars. But rather than helping people condemned to poverty by misfortune, Ruthven aided those who begged, not to ease their circumstances, but to drown themselves further in excesses. Moreover the vagabonds helped by Lord Ruthven seemed to be cursed, as they were invariably victims of some mishap.

In Aubrey's heightened imagination, all this took on a supernatural quality that disturbed him more each day. He didn't like his friend's fondness for drink and gambling, either, and he was even less fond of the way Lord Ruthven involved innocent young people in this behavior. One day, sick of the whole thing, Aubrey told the noble that he intended to travel on alone.

AUBREY IN GREECE

After separating from Lord Ruthven, Aubrey went to Greece. In Athens he stayed in the home of a man whose daughter was the most beautiful girl Aubrey had ever seen. Ianthe, as she was called, often accompanied Aubrey on his walks in the forest, or when he visited ancient monuments. It was the girl's innocence that most attracted the lad. Little by little he became more attached to her, and one day he realized that the sweet Ianthe had conquered his heart.

Unfortunately, Aubrey knew that no one in London would approve the marriage of an upper-class Englishman to a Greek peasant girl. He needed to consider his predicament, so he planned a solitary excursion in search of archaeological remains in order to distract himself from thoughts of the young woman.

When Ianthe and her family learned what forest Aubrey intended to visit, they were horrified and begged him to return before sunset.

"That place is frequented by vampires at night," Ianthe's father assured him. "Anyone who dares cross their path falls under the most terrible evil."

Ianthe had already told Aubrey stories of vampires. He'd heard the legends of the region, but he did not believe them. The only thing that made him uncomfortable was that Ianthe's description of these creatures was an exact match for Lord Ruthven's appearance.

AUBREY'S EXCURSION

Refusing to be put off by superstition, Aubrey set out on his excursion. The day went well, but when thunder began rumbling overhead, he realized he had stayed longer than he'd intended. In the gloom he spotted a cottage where he might take shelter until the rain ended. As he approached, he heard chilling screams and saw a shadowy figure flee into the forest. Aubrey entered, and to his horror, he found a woman lying on the floor. He advanced toward her as a lightning flash lit up the beautiful, lifeless face of his beloved. On her throat she bore the unmistakable bite marks of a vampire. Beside her was a dagger.

THE RETURN OF LORD RUTHVEN

After Ianthe's death, Aubrey fell ill and was bedridden for several months. By strange coincidence, Lord Ruthven arrived in Athens around that time. On learning about his friend's illness, he insisted on moving into the house to care for him – day and night.

At first, Aubrey was horrified to see the person whose face he had associated with a vampire's. But little by little, with kind words and dedicated nursing, Lord Ruthven completely won back the young man's trust. In fact, when he recovered, Aubrey insisted that they resume their travels and visit the rest of Greece together.

The two men set off again, but before long, some bandits attacked them and mortally wounded Lord Ruthven. With his dying breath he uttered these words:

"Talk to no one of my sins or my death. Swear you will not say I am dead."

Devastated by his friend's murder, Aubrey promised, "I swear."

THE WEIGHT OF THE OATH

Tired of a country that had brought him such misfortune, Aubrey decided to return to London, but first, he had to sort out Lord Ruthven's belongings. He shuddered when he found an empty dagger sheath. The bloody weapon found beside Ianthe's body fitted perfectly into it.

Aubrey reached London just in time to attend his sister's coming of age party. She was being presented to society in the very same salon where Aubrey had first met Lord Ruthven.

While Aubrey watched his sister, someone grasped his arm and whispered, "Remember your oath!" He turned and almost fainted at the sight of Lord Ruthven standing before him. Paralyzed, Aubrey saw Ruthven approach his sister. Both conversed happily until the end of the party. Aubrey tried to talk to his sister after the party, but he could only mutter senseless phrases, while a voice in his head constantly warned: "Remember your oath."

Aubrey was ill for months and nearly went mad. His sister was engaged to be married and brought him a portrait of her fiancé. Aubrey thought he would die when he saw the face of the dreaded Ruthven, for now there was no doubt he was a vampire.

In vain Aubrey tried to get his sister to cancel the wedding, but he was still unable to reveal that her intended had risen from the grave.

The wedding was held, and as the clock struck midnight, Aubrey struggled from his sickbed and hastened to his sister's house. He was too late. There was no trace of Lord Ruthven, but his new wife lay pale and lifeless on the bed. On her beautiful neck, the mark of a bite left no room for doubt: Aubrey's sister had satisfied the vampire's thirst for blood.

end

The Pale Lady

Alexandre Dumas

(France, 1802-1870)

FLEEING FROM WAR

I was born in Sandomir, Poland. My story opens in 1825, when one of those wars that seems intent on draining all the blood from two nations was raging between Russia and Poland. My father had led an uprising against the new Tsar, and now there were barely a hundred knights left of the thirty thousand he'd had under his command at the start.

One day, he chose ten of those hundred men and asked them to take me to a convent in the heart of the Carpathian Mountains. It was a very difficult place to reach, and there I would be protected.

THE ATTACK

On the tenth day of our journey, we were nearing our destination, when suddenly the noise of firearms rang out. Some thirty bandits appeared on the hillside. Some attacked us head-on, while others cut off our retreat. When only four of my guards were left, the leader of the thieves shouted an order and I understood my time had come. I whispered a prayer and, before fainting, glimpsed a young man riding at full speed down the hill.

When I came to, I was in the arms of the young man, who was arguing in French with the leader of the attack.

"Kostakis, withdraw your men at once. I will allow you to rule in the castle, but I govern the forest. And this young woman is under my care."

"I accept, Gregorisk, but only if you agree that the young lady be taken to the castle. She is beautiful, and I want her for myself."

"I will lead her to the castle, but I will deliver her to our mother, and I will not abandon her," my protector replied.

LIFE IN THE CASTLE

I soon learned that the two brothers had the same mother, Princess Smeranda, but different fathers. Gregorisk, blond and with lovely blue eyes, was the legitimate son of a Slavic prince. Kostakis, with his fierce black eyes, was the illegitimate child of a half Greek, half Moldavian Count.

Their mother welcomed me warmly to the castle, and treated me like a daughter. Soon it became clear that both brothers were in love with me.

I preferred Gregorisk. Smeranda, however, clearly favored her son Kostakis. Every night, on giving me a goodnight kiss on the forehead, she whispered in French, so that I could understand: "Kostakis loves Eduvigis!"

GREGORISK'S PLAN

One night, when I had just retired, someone
knocked softly on my bedroom door. It was Gregorisk.

"Our lives depend on this conversation," he said. I took his hand, as
my heart pounded. "I love you. I need to know if you love me and want to
be my wife."

"Yes, I love you!" I told him.

"Then you know that we will not be safe unless we flee from here. Tomorrow night I'll hide two horses in the fields behind the castle. We will leave by
the kitchen door and escape into the countryside to begin our lives together."

We sealed our pact with a kiss and said good-bye. I was frightened, but at the same time, my heart was overflowing with happiness. I was about to become the wife of the man I loved.

WHERE IS YOUR BROTHER?

The next morning, Gregorisk left the castle to go about his business, saying he would return at dusk, as usual. As he left the room, his brother's eyes followed him with such blazing hatred that I shuddered.

I was restless all day. By dinnertime neither brother had returned. Finally, I heard footsteps, and a shape loomed out of the darkness.

It was my love! But he was as pale as a corpse, and on seeing him I knew something terrible had happened.

"Where is your brother?" his mother asked.

"Oh, mother," Gregorisk answered, his voice trembling. "I do not know, as we weren't together, but his horse has just entered the castle yard, alone and stained with blood."

VENGEANCE

Kostakis's body was found in the forest and brought back to the castle. Smeranda kneeled beside it and called Gregorisk to her.

"My son," she said. "I need to know that you will kill Kostakis's murderer. Swear you will avenge him!"

Gregorisk put his hand on the corpse and said, "I swear the murderer will die!"

As those words were uttered, I saw the eyes of the corpse open and stare, more fierce and alive than ever, into mine. I felt faint, but Smeranda noticed and took my trembling hand.

Alone in my bedchamber I lay, terrified, yet suddenly exhausted. Eventually, I fell into a deep sleep.

In the morning I awoke feeling weak and with a sore neck. I looked in the mirror and was shocked by my pale reflection. Two small marks on my neck, looked almost like insect bites.

A Vampire's Kiss

Each morning for days I had the same symptoms. Weakened, I spent all of my time in bed. One morning Gregorisk came to me, thinking I no longer loved him. He said that life without me would be unbearable, and that he was thinking of retiring to a monastery. I swore I loved him still and explained what had been happening to me since Kostakis's death.

"He must be a vampire," he murmured. On hearing from his lips the fear that was already nesting in my soul, I burst into tears. He embraced me and swore he knew how to defeat his brother.

That very day we married secretly, and the priest gave Gregorisk a holy sword. That evening, while I pretended to sleep, Gregorisk hid behind my bed.

Late into the night the door creaked open, and Kostakis appeared. He was as pale as a corpse, and blood flowed from his mortal wound.

As he drew close to me, Gregorisk appeared, brandishing his weapon. "I am not to blame for your death!" he shouted. "It was you who threw yourself on my sword that night. Your unholy mission is finished. You left your grave as a vampire, but tonight you will return to it for all eternity!"

With these words, Gregorisk plunged the sacred sword into his brother's heart. With an unnatural shriek, Kostakis cried out and then lay still. His reign of terror was over.

end

Vampire's Honor

Arabian Tale
from *The Thousand and One Nights*

THE LOUSE SKIN

When she was very little, Princess Dalal, the beautiful child of a sultan, found a louse on her head. With great care, the girl put it into a big jar full of oil and closed the lid. She did not know that oil causes surprising changes to these tiny creatures. Forgotten in its jar, the louse grew from year to year. When the princess was sixteen, the beast burst out of the jar and fled. With its great size and curved horns, it resembled a buffalo. The palace guards captured it and brought it before the sultan, who said this to the princess:

"Beloved daughter, as it is time you were married, I will have this creature killed. We will hang its skin at the palace gate and the first young man who realizes it comes from what was once a bloodthirsty little insect, will win your hand. Everyone who guesses wrong will lose his head."

Many young men paraded before the palace. Some said "It's a buffalo skin," and lost their heads. "A mountain goat's skin," others said, and they too, were sorry. Much blood was spilled until the most handsome young man of all arrived and said: "It's the skin of a louse grown in oil."

THE VAMPIRE'S WIFE

Dalal was married, but to what, no one knew. As it turned out, the handsome young man was the worst kind of vampire.

Dalal lived in terror, but did not dare run away. One day the vampire decided to test her. Using his magic powers, he took on the form of Dalal's mother and knocked at their front door.

"My daughter, we have discovered that your husband is a vampire. I'm here to rescue you. Come and escape with me!"

Dalal was deeply moved by her mother's courage, but was afraid of what the vampire might do. To protect her mother, Dalal decided to lie:

"What are you saying, mother? There are no vampires here. Please don't dishonor my dear husband!"

WOUNDED PRIDE

The vampire was satisfied to see that his wife had not betrayed him, but to be sure of her loyalty, he decided to test her once more. This time he appeared before Dalal as the Sultan himself and said:

"Beloved daughter, I am distressed, as news has reached me that you have married a vampire. I beg you to say it isn't so."

Dalal could not hold in her secret any longer and confessed to her father all the horrible things the vampire did.

"I am truly frightened he will eventually kill me, too, Father."

When she finished these words, the false Sultan turned into the enraged vampire, who roared and showed his horrific fangs, intending to devour his wife on the spot.

"Don't eat me now, dear husband," shouted Dalal, who was a very smart princess, "as I am dirty, and my flesh would not taste sweet. Take me to the baths where the women go to clean and perfume themselves, and I will emerge as a much more appetizing morsel."

THE CHESTNUT SELLER

The vampire took Dalal to the baths where the women were making themselves beautiful.

Once inside with the other women, Dalal beckoned to an old lady. "Come here, Grandma," she said. "Will you give me your chestnut basket and rags in exchange for my fine clothes and all the jewelry I'm wearing?"

The old woman was delighted to accept, and Dalal hurriedly dressed in her rags. Disguised as a chestnut seller, she left the baths and marched right past her vampire husband without his suspecting a thing.

Much later, by the time the vampire realized he had been tricked, Dalal was far away and safe, which was lucky for her, indeed.

THE RAM

Many months after Dalal's safe return to her family, she met a young prince and was about to be married. But on the morning of the wedding, a huge white ram appeared at the palace gate.

When Dalal saw the ram, she immediately knew it was one of the vampire's disguises. In tears, she fled to lock herself in her room and to plead with the goddess Zeinab for mercy. The goddess took pity on her and sent a guardian spirit to protect her.

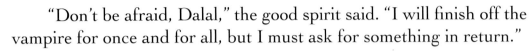

"Don't be afraid, Dalal," the good spirit said. "I will finish off the vampire for once and for all, but I must ask for something in return."

"I'll do whatever you want," Dalal promised.

"My son is very ill. If he is to recover, he must drink a cup of water from the Emerald Sea," the spirit explained. "I am only a spirit and cannot fill the cup, which is why I must ask this favor of you. But be warned. The Sultan of the Emerald Sea forbids anyone to take even one drop of the precious water."

THE EMERALD SEA

As soon as the vampire was dead, the princess and the guardian spirit left for the Emerald Sea. There, Dalal filled a cup with water and gave it to the spirit. But as she was doing so, a wave wet her hand, which turned as green as clover.

Years later, when vampires and cups of water were all but forgotten, a genie offering emerald bangles and rings arrived at the palace. Like the other women, Dalal wanted to try on a bracelet.

"Princess, I do not place my goods on the left hand," the genie said on seeing that Dalal hid her other hand.

When Dalal timidly revealed her green hand, the genie knew she had stolen the sea water. He took her straight to the Sultan. But when the Sultan heard her story, he did not punish Dalal. Instead, he asked the princess if he might marry her eldest daughter. The two met, and in time, the young princess and the Sultan of the Emerald Sea were married. The royal families were joined, and everyone lived happily to the end of their days.

end

The Dancing Vampire

A.N. Afanasiev

(Russia, 1826-1871)

MARUSSIA AT THE DANCE

In a certain kingdom of a certain nation lived an elderly couple with a daughter named Marussia. In that kingdom it was the custom to hold a joyful, week-long festival each spring. On this particular occasion, the village girls met in a cabin and prepared all the food and drinks they would need for the festivities. In the evening, the boys arrived, and the fun and dancing began.

On the first night, a very attractive young stranger with pale skin came to the cabin. No one knew where he was from, but he was polite and sociable and was liked immediately. When he started to dance, he was admired too, because his dancing was a genuine marvel. Since Marussia was the best dancer among the girls, everyone encouraged her to be his partner.

At the party's end, the gentleman offered to accompany Marussia home. Before saying good-bye, he said, "Marussia, though we have just met, I love you and want to ask you to become my wife. Will you marry me?"

Marussia was very pleased at the young man's declaration because she, too, felt love stirring within her. At the same time, she was quite surprised as this was very sudden. And when she asked where he was from and what he did, the mysterious stranger was evasive and really didn't answer at all.

THE BALL OF THREAD

At home, Marussia immediately told her mother everything that had happened, expressing both her excitement and her doubts.

"Listen, Marussia," her mother said. "Take a ball of thread with you tomorrow. When you say goodnight to this fellow, tie the thread to one of his buttons without his noticing. Then you will be able to follow the thread and discover where he lives."

Marussia did as her mother said. Shortly after parting with the young man, she followed the thread she had tied to his coat button, and it led her to the church. On entering, she saw her fiancé leaning over a coffin, draining the blood from a corpse!

Marussia fled in terror and could not even manage to tell her mother what had happened. The following night, her mother insisted she return to the festival. After the festivities, though Marussia tried to avoid him, the young man sought her out and accompanied her to her door where he asked, "Did you follow me to the church yesterday?"

Marussia hurriedly denied it. Then the vampire (for that's what he was) warned her: "If you're lying, you will die tomorrow night."

THE WISE GRANDMOTHER

Marussia went to bed extremely frightened, but on waking, she remembered that her grandmother, though very old, was also very wise. She paid her a visit at once and told her everything in detail. Her grandmother knew exactly what to do.

"Go to see the priest at once, and tell him that should you die, you wish to be buried at the crossroad. Don't be afraid, little one. When the time comes, you will rise again."

That night Marissa did die and later was buried at the crossroad. A few days later, a noble and his servant came to her grave. They stopped and were surprised to find an exquisite flower growing on top of it.

"This is the most beautiful flower I have ever seen," the noble said. "Let's dig it up, root and all, and plant it in a flower pot."

The Awakening of a Flower

The little flower grew more beautiful each day. One night, when the noble could not sleep, he got up and went into the garden where the pot with the beautiful flower stood. When midnight struck, something extraordinary happened. First, the flower began to move, swaying from side to side. Then, it fell from its stalk to the ground. Before the incredulous eyes of the noble, the flower stopped being a flower and turned into the most beautiful young woman he had ever seen. Of course, this young woman was none other than Marussia.

The noble begged her to marry him as soon as possible, and Marussia gave her consent – on one condition.

"Promise me that for four years you won't ask me to go to the church."

The noble accepted the strange request, and soon they were wed in a beautiful meadow and were both very happy.

The Broken Promise

Two years later, Marussia and her husband had a baby boy. Her husband insisted they have the child christened, and Marussia agreed to go to the church.

That same night, the vampire appeared beside her bed and asked, "Have you been inside the church?"

Afraid, Marussia denied it, but before leaving the vampire whispered, "If you have lied to me, your husband and son will die."

The End of the Curse

In the morning, Marussia ran to her grandmother to ask her advice once more. Her grandmother gave her one small vial of holy water and another containing the water of life. Then she told Marussia what to do.

After dark, the vampire appeared and snatched away the lives of both Marussia's husband and son. But Marussia confronted him with these words:

"Yesterday I was in the church, and I was there the first time you asked me, too. That was when I saw you drink a corpse's blood and discovered you are a vampire."

Immediately, she sprinkled the monster with holy water and he turned to dust that instant. Then she ran to her husband and infant, sprinkled them with the water of life, and watched as they came back to life, just as she had. From that day on, Marussia and her family lived together with no further troubles for many, many years.

end

The Family of the Vurdalak

A.K. Tolstoy

(Russia, 1817-1875)

A STORY OF TERROR

More than likely you enjoy hearing horror stories. Once I liked to listen to them, too, but I always thought they lacked one essential ingredient: authenticity.

Now, I know one such terrible – and true tale. Not only that, I didn't just hear the story. Unfortunately, I played the lead role in it.

It occurred in 1759. That year I was in love with a woman who didn't feel any love for me. Therefore, I decided to seek a diplomatic post in Moldavia, so as to move as far away from her as possible.

I spoke Serbian well enough to be understood, and one day on my journey, I reached a town where I hoped to find accommodation in some family's home. I knocked on the first door I found and quickly saw that the inhabitants of the house were deeply upset.

"Come in, stranger," a man who was about thirty said. "Don't be disturbed by our sadness. When I tell you what's wrong, you'll understand."

Then he told me that his elderly father, a man named Gorcha, had gone into the mountains to hunt down a bandit and had told him:

"If it takes me more than ten days to return home, don't let me in. If this happens, I order you to forget who I am and to plunge a stake into my heart, as it would mean that I had turned into a cursed Vurdalak and had come to suck your blood."

THE VURDALAKS

At this point, I should tell you that the Vurdalaks are vampires of the Slavic peoples; corpses who, like all vampires, have left their tombs to suck the blood of the living, but with a characteristic that makes them still more sinister. Vurdalaks prefer to suck the blood of their most intimate friends and family.

My arrival in the village coincided precisely when the term of ten days set by Gorcha expired, which was why the family was in such anguish.

"What time did Dad leave?" Peter asked his brother, George.

"At eight, and now it's half past seven."

The whole family was gathered at the window, anxiously watching the path. Peter, George, and sweet Sdenka were Gorcha's three children. George's wife and their two children were there too.

Just as the clock struck eight, we spotted a figure emerge from the forest and head toward us.

"It's him," Peter and his sister-in-law exclaimed happily.

"Yes, but… how do we know if the ten days have gone by or not?" George asked.

THE RETURN OF GORCHA

The old man entered the house and looked at us all with sunken, lifeless eyes.

"Aren't you going to receive me as I deserve?" he complained. "Perhaps you haven't noticed that I am wounded."

In fact, the old man had a wound on the left side of his chest. George's wife put on some bandages and brought him food.

George watched his father with distrust all the while, and I have to admit, I went to bed deeply affected by the terrible appearance of the old man and by his disagreeable manners. In the middle of the night, I awoke suddenly, convinced someone was watching me. Through the window, I saw Gorcha's face pressed against the glass. Then he went to the window of the room beside mine, and I heard him call the youngest of his grandchildren.

"Grandad, if I come out, will you explain how you fought the bandit?"

"Of course, darling. But try not to make any noise when you open the window, because we don't want your father to wake up and get angry."

THE GRANDFATHER AND THE CHILD

That dialogue made my hair stand up on end, but I was strangely paralyzed and unable to call out for help. At least I managed to bang on the wall of the next room with all my strength. When at last I recovered my voice and began to shout, everyone in the house awoke. Too late: I had seen the old man pass in front of my window with the boy in his arms.

George ran off toward the forest and after several hours returned with the child. George had found him, unconscious, on the path, but the boy didn't seem to have been harmed. He told us he had been playing with his grandfather and he didn't remember why he had fainted. Though we searched everywhere for Gorcha, we could not find him: he had disappeared.

A few days later I had to continue on my journey to the city of Jassy. I left very worried about the child who, after the incident with his grandfather, had woken up sick the next morning. I was also sad to say good-bye to Sdenka, as my affection for the sweet, Slavic beauty was growing.

The Plague of Vampirism

Six months later, I started my return journey home, but before leaving, I wanted to see Sdenka and her family again. On reaching the town, I noticed that the monastery was full of pilgrims.

"Isn't there any lodging left in the village?" I asked a priest.

"On the contrary," he told me. "Thanks to the cursed Gorcha, the place is all but empty."

"Is Gorcha still alive?"

"Oh, no! He lies dead with a stake through his heart, but he sucked the blood of George's son, and the son then sucked the blood of his mother, and so on, until the whole family and practically the entire town was infected with vampirism. The plague is contagious."

"Sdenka too?" I asked with a knot in my heart.

"No, I don't think so. The poor girl went mad with grief, but I believe she managed to escape."

I left the priest in mid-sentence and ran to George's house, hoping to find some clue as to Sdenka's whereabouts.

The town was empty and silent, and all the windows were dark. On reaching George's house, I found the door open, but all the rooms were empty. The only signs of life were in Sdenka's room: a dress, some jewels, the tangled sheets. I was exhausted and distraught. I stretched out on the bed and fell into a troubled sleep.

Meeting Sdenka Again

I awoke from a nightmare, confused and disoriented to find Sdenka beside my bed. She was lovelier than ever.

"Why did you leave, my darling?" she said. "Can't you see I love you more than my own soul, and your life belongs to me?"

There was nothing left of the sweet, shy girl I remembered. I wanted to embrace this beautiful woman who was caressing me, but something stopped me.

"Sdenka, where is the holy cross you always wore around your neck?" I asked.

"I lost it," she answered nervously. "But hold me, my love, and let me kiss you."

Sdenka's face was as pale as death, and now the sickening smell of badly closed graves filled the room.

"I will spend the night with you, my love," I lied. "But first, let me get the gift I brought for you. It's in my saddlebag."

I reached the stable, leapt on my horse, and galloped away from that place as fast as the poor beast could carry me. Not only Sdenka, but old Gorcha, George, Peter, the children, and their mother all followed me for a while, shouting my name. That disastrous adventure killed my desire to travel and find romance forever. Those who know me understand very well why I have led such a tranquil and solitary life since.

end

Vampirism

E.T.A. Hoffmann

(Germany, 1776-1822)

An Unexpected Visit

After long journeys through distant lands, Count Hippolyte returned home to claim his father's rich legacy. He restored his castle magnificently, inspired by the art and beauty he had seen in his world travels.

One morning, the arrival of an elderly baroness, a very distant relative, was announced. On hearing her name, Hippolyte remembered how much his father had disliked this woman. However, his father had never explained why he had such an aversion to her. In the village there had always been malicious gossip that connected the baroness to some terrible crime.

Nevertheless, the young count received her, not only out of good hospitality, but because he thought that village rumors were entirely baseless.

When the elderly woman entered, Hippolyte was taken aback, so repugnant was the expression on her face. But, on turning away, he saw the delectable creature accompanying her. The young woman's sweetness and beauty struck him dumb.

"I regret that your father was so influenced by certain ideas about me that my enemies have been in the habit of spreading," said the baroness with the utmost politeness. "However, I always held him in the greatest esteem."

Blinded by the young woman's beauty – introduced by the baroness as her daughter, Aurelia – the count begged the old lady to stay at the castle for a few days, by way of apologizing for his dead father's rudeness.

The Death of the Baroness

Very soon, Hippolyte felt that destiny had placed in his path the only woman in the world whom he could love enough to make his bride. He was happy in Aurelia's company, and it was not so very difficult to become accustomed to the frightening spectral face of her elderly mother. The baroness also suffered strange fits of illness, during which she remained paralyzed so that it was impossible not to confuse her with a corpse!

On the very morning when Hippolyte thought to confess his love to Aurelia and ask for her hand, the lifeless body of the baroness was found near the cemetery. Curiously, this was the place chosen by the old lady for her frequent night-time strolls.

Aurelia was devastated by the blow, and though the count did not want to rush a decision of marriage at such a time, he needed to tell her of his love and desire to marry. To his surprise, Aurelia reacted by flinging herself into his arms and shouting:

"For the love of God and the salvation of my soul, let's get married as soon as possible!"

AURELIA'S CONFESSION

Though some time had elapsed since the wedding, Aurelia's anxiety did not diminish. She loved the count, as he did her, but in the middle of their sweetest and most loving conversations, she would often turn pale and embrace her husband as if victim of some unimaginable fear. One night, Hippolyte asked Aurelia as gently as possible about her fears. To his utter surprise he learned that the cause of such great anguish was her mother's perversity.

"Is there anything more terrible than having your own mother as an enemy?" the young woman lamented. She told Hippolyte of her terrible childhood and adolescence. From an early age, Aurelia had had to live with her mother and her mother's lover, a violent and coarse man. The situation became so unbearable that one day Aurelia tried to run away. Then her mother locked her in a room and gave her nothing to eat all day. In the end, the baroness's lover turned out to be a well-known murderer, who was arrested and hanged. Because of the scandal, the baroness had had to leave the area, along with her daughter, which is how the two of them had reached the count's castle.

Aurelia was happy when love for Hippolyte began to grow and told her mother. But her mother reacted with one of her attacks of madness and violence.

"Since your birth, when you caused me pain, you have brought me nothing but misfortune. If you marry, my vengeance will reach you in the middle of your dreamed-of happiness."

Aurelia threw herself into the count's arms on recalling those terrifying words. He trembled almost as much as she did, on learning of the baroness's monstrous character.

THE STRANGE ILLNESS

Confessing to her husband what she had kept secret for so long seemed to calm Aurelia somewhat. However, after some months of happy marriage, she began to behave very strangely, and she looked ill with faded eyes and extremely pale skin. She avoided her husband and spent hours locked away in her room. Sometimes she went on long walks, from which she always returned with eyes red from crying and her face pinched with anguish.

The count tried to find out what frightful torment was assailing her, but every attempt to talk with her was fruitless. No doctors were able to say what was happening to her.

Most disturbing of all was that Aurelia refused to eat. Everything repelled her, especially meat. The very sight of it forced her to leave the table. After several months, no one understood how Aurelia was still living, since she lacked any sustenance.

E.T.A. HOFFMANN

THE WITCHES' HOUR

The revelations of a servant added to the count's concern.

"Sir, I do not wish to be indiscreet, but I think it is time you knew that Countess Aurelia leaves the castle every night and does not return till dawn."

On hearing this, the count shuddered. For some time now he had been feeling strangely fatigued every night and slept so deeply that it didn't seem natural. Till then he had attributed this to extreme nervous exhaustion, but now he wondered whether Aurelia was giving him some drug in the tea she prepared for him every night at bedtime.

He decided to find out that same evening. When his wife served him the drink, he thanked her, but did not touch a drop. He went to bed at the usual time, but this time felt no deep sleepiness. He pretended to slumber, and shortly the countess got up and left the bedroom.

Hippolyte followed Aurelia to the park and through the cemetery gates. What he saw by the clear light of the moon froze the blood in his veins. Wicked, half-naked old crones were dragging the corpse of a man along the ground, while various other hags were engaged in devouring it like ravenous wolves. Worse still, Aurelia was among them!

The count fled as best he could on trembling legs, trying in vain to wipe the horrific scene from his mind. His beloved wife was a cursed vampire!

Before dawn Hippolyte saddled his horse and rode as far away from his castle and all his wealth as he could. No one ever saw him again, but some say he went mad and lived out his days in torment.

end

Thanathopia

Rubén Darío

(Nicaragua, 1867-1916)

THE FEARS OF JAMES LEEN

"You ridicule me for what you call my childish fears, but I'm not offended, because I know your disbelief is the result of ignorance." James Leen rested his elbows on the bar where several men were looking at him in amusement. "I'm not mad or drunk, and I'm not ashamed to admit that cemeteries, the dark, abandoned houses, and nightwoods with flying bats frighten me. If you have the patience to listen, I'll tell you a story that explains why."

"Let's have it then, James!" urged one of the listeners.

"Yes, come on, tell us," the rest chimed in.

"The first thing you should know is that before escaping to Argentina, I was held prisoner for five years by my own father, the respected Dr. John Leen, Fellow of the Royal Society for Psychic Research in London. On his orders I was committed to a lunatic asylum, because he was afraid I would reveal what he wanted to keep hidden. And that is what I am going to tell you tonight. I've waited a long time to tell the truth, and I can stay silent no longer.

JAMES LEEN TELLS HIS STORY

"When I was a child, my mother died, and my father sent me at once to a boarding-school in Oxford. My father never showed me any affection and came to visit me only once a year. As I grew, I became more and more melancholy and lonely. Although I was still very young, I had learned everything there was to know about sadness.

"One day, a visit from my father was announced. I remember needing to unburden myself to someone so badly that I received him with joy, even though his coldness toward me over the years had turned my heart against him.

"Although Father avoided looking directly at me, I was surprised to note he seemed much friendlier than on previous occasions. And when I told him that my studies had concluded and I wanted to return to London, his reply surprised me even more:

"'I was already planning on taking you with me today. I wanted to tell you that it was high time I had the support of a family again, and I've remarried. You have a new stepmother, and she wants to meet you.'

"A stepmother! When I heard that, the image of my own, sweet mother came to mind. I remembered how she suffered when my father abandoned her to spend day and night shut up in his laboratory. I remained silent as I packed my bags in order to leave with my father.

THE RETURN HOME

"On our arrival at the London mansion, I was disappointed to learn that all of the old servants that I had been fond of were gone. In their place were five thin old people, pale and ill-looking, who bowed as we passed with ridiculous formality.

"All of my mother's things had been replaced with austere and uncomfortable furnishings. Everything about the house created a hostile and gloomy atmosphere.

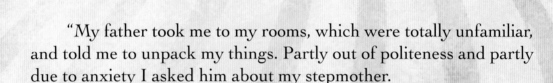

"My father took me to my rooms, which were totally unfamiliar, and told me to unpack my things. Partly out of politeness and partly due to anxiety I asked him about my stepmother.

"'Don't be in such a hurry, dear James, you'll meet her soon enough,' he answered. 'As I told you before, she is eager to get to know you.'

"Father had never called me 'dear James.' His reply and the whole dismal atmosphere of that place made me feel more anxious by the minute. I tried to rest a while on my bed as the train journey had been long, but despite an unnatural weariness in my body and soul, I could not get to sleep. A few hours later, I heard my father's footsteps approaching.

"He opened the door and looked directly into my eyes for the first time ever, and when he did so, I almost cried out in alarm, for those eyes were utterly indescribable."

"Come on, James, try. Tell us what they were like," said the owner of the bar, who had joined the group of listeners.

"The irises were red, like a rabbit's," James continued.
"Yes, they were rabbit eyes that stared so intensely that I trembled uncontrollably.

The Stepmother

"'Come on, son,' my father told me, 'your stepmother is waiting. She is ready to meet you now.'

"I desperately wanted to flee. I had a premonition that I was about to confront danger. We went down to the sitting room, and there, in a high-backed chair, a woman was waiting. I was afraid to look at her, but my father said:

"'Come closer, dear James, and greet your new mother.'

"I approached, and still unable to meet her gaze, I held out my hand to the woman. On touching that hand, my whole body trembled and an icy chill penetrated the very marrow of my bones. I swear that her cold, stiff hand, didn't belong to anyone of this world.

"'Look at me, dear James,' the specter said.

"I slowly raised my eyes, and, ridiculous as it may sound, my teeth began to chatter from pure terror. I clenched my jaw to repress a scream and willed myself to stare directly at her. Her eyes were not human. They had no shine at all. They were the eyes of a corpse! And the smell – it was the putrid stench of death!

"'Come closer, my son,' the purple lips on the face of that corpse intoned. 'I want to kiss you.'

"'No,' I screamed with all the strength in my body. 'I'm leaving here, and I'll tell the whole world that Dr. Leen is a crazed killer and that his wife is a vampire! Yes, my father's a madman who is married to a vampire!'"

Having told the truth at last, James Leen fell unconscious at the bar. And now to be certain, there were no jokes, there was no ridicule. Not one smile of disbelief could be seen on the lips of the men listening. Such a dense silence followed that one could almost hear the chattering of teeth.

end

This section of the book contains legends in the folk tradition that travel around the world from mouth to ear, person to person, and country to country. Whatever their age or land of origin, they have one thing in common: they are about the adventures and evil deeds of those nocturnal beings we all know as vampires.

Li-Yung and the Vampire. This legend has been told in China since the earliest imperial dynasties. A bold, smart child discovers that a vampire with a fox's tail is causing his mother's mysterious illness. Only he dares to challenge and destroy this being and its fellows. Yes, China has its vampire stories, too!

The Vampire Witch. Galicia is a community in Spain, rich in the tradition of storytelling. Legends about witches, magical spells, and sinister beings – including vampires – have always been popular. The protagonists of this story are a girl and a vampire witch who turns into a black fly. The legend claims that vampire witches are experts at becoming nearly invisible to human eyes. Don't doubt it for a moment, especially if you hear that familiar *buzzzz* in your ear!

Mount Wawel Castle. This is a fascinating legend from Poland about a vampire who wouldn't allow anyone to live in his castle. If you want to find out what happened to anyone who tried to spend a weekend in Mount Wawel Castle, just read on – if you dare.

The Warriors of the Crypt. In Denmark in the Middle Ages, a man named Saxo Grammaticus may have penned a legend that spread throughout Europe. It is the story of two friends who vowed to remain together even in death. But the forces of evil converted this friendship into an unparalleled battle between a living friend and a bloodthirsty vampire.

Vampire
Legends

Li-Yung and the Vampire

The Vampire Witch

Mount Wawel Castle

The Warriors of the Crypt

Li-Yung and the Vampire

ancient chinese legend

AN ANGUISHED MOTHER

The father of Li-Yung was a busy trader who often had to go on long journeys. Sometimes he was gone for months, leaving Li-Yung, who was only twelve, in the care of his mother and the elderly servant woman, Ching.

On one such journey, Li-Yung's father went to sell cloth in the distant mountains of the West. Four months later he had not returned, and Li-Yung's mother was absolutely desperate. She became convinced that her husband had been eaten by a bear. She spent her days worrying and found it hard to sleep at night. Even when she did manage to sleep, she woke up in the middle of the night shouting, "It's here! It's here! Get it out of my room!"

"What's here?" the alarmed child and servant asked. But the poor woman did not know how to explain. She was just certain that someone had entered her bedroom at night.

FOX HAIRS

Li-Yung was very worried about his mother, who was becoming paler and weaker, as if afflicted by some strange disease. One day, the boy found fox hairs by the door of his mother's bedroom. At once he showed them to the elderly Ching to see what she thought.

"There's no doubt in my mind," the old woman said. "A vampire with a fox's tail visits your mother every night."

Li-Yung took the biggest and sharpest knife from the kitchen, and, without her knowledge, he hid under his mother's bed, ready to defend her from the beast then and there.

THE TAIL TORN OFF

Unfortunately, Li-Yung fell asleep. Even so, at midnight a noise awoke him. He sprang out from under the bed just in time to raise his knife and bring it down with all his strength as the vampire fled from the room. He heard a terrible shriek as the creature disappeared.

Old Ching rushed in and lit the lamps. There, lying on the floor, was a splendid fox tail that Li-Yung had managed to cut off the vampire.

THE VAMPIRE'S YARD

"I know of a yard behind the cemetery," old Ching told Li-Yung. "They say it's the place where the vampire-foxes meet."

When the sun set, Li-Yung went to the yard and hid behind a tree. A few hours later, three men appeared. Two were tall, robust, and elegantly dressed, but the third was old and bent – undoubtedly a servant. The two had fox tails, which is to say, vampire tails. The third one without a tail said, "I'm ashamed for you to see me looking like this."

"If I had for a lover as beautiful a woman as you have, I wouldn't worry about my tail in the least," the first man said to cheer him up.

"And what kind of servant are you that you haven't even got a glass of blood to offer us?" chided the second man.

THE TRICK

Li-Yung could listen no more. He hurried home and jumped into bed, absolutely furious at these vampire-foxes. In the morning, he asked old Ching to sew the severed fox's tail to his trousers. She did so, all the while begging him to take great care with whatever he was planning to do.

Li-Yung bought a bottle of the darkest red wine he could find and for several nights roamed the area near the cemetery in search of the old servant. When at last he found him, Li-Yung raised his coat and showed his tail.

"Are you new here?" the vampire inquired.

"Yes, I've arrived only recently. I'm so lonely that I wanted to share this very special bottle of blood with you and your friends. Perhaps it will open the doors of friendship," Li-Yung answered.

The old man was only too delighted to invite Li-Yung to meet his masters the following night, and to share the bottle of "blood" with them, of course.

LI-YUNG, HIS FATHER, AND THE POISON

While all this was happening, Li-Yung's father, who did not believe in vampire-foxes or vampires of any kind for that matter, had at last returned from his journey. Upon seeing the condition of his wife he called for the best doctors in the city.

"It's most peculiar," they said. "This woman has no disease, yet she is dying."

The following night, Li-Yung had to go and meet the vampires at the yard, and he asked his father to accompany him.

Father and son went to the yard and, hidden, they watched as those men with foxes' tails appeared, carrying the bottle of blood-red wine.

"When do you think the young vampire who gave you the blood will arrive?" one of them asked the servant. "He's late and I am thirsty. Let's have a toast in his honor while we wait."

The three vampires emptied their glasses in one gulp. As Li-Yung had hoped, they immediately began to writhe in pain because everything that is not blood is poison for a vampire. Before father and son, they dissolved and vanished!

PROSPERITY

At the very moment that the vampires disappeared, the mother of Li-Yung said to the elderly servant, "How strange! I dreamed I was a burning candle, and someone put out the flame that was consuming me."

From then on, she recovered her health and the happiness she had known before. Li-Yung's father stayed home with his wife. Now it was Li-Yung who traveled.

"You are no longer a child, as you have shown you have the wisdom of a sage," his father said.

The family businesses prospered greatly, and thanks to Li-Yung, good luck shone brightly on them for a very long time.

end

The Vampire Witch

Galician Legend

AN UNFORTUNATE MARRIED COUPLE

A long time ago now, in the Spanish village of San Xián de Sergude, lived a most unfortunate married couple. They were unlucky because all of their children died shortly after being born. It always happened in the same way. The baby would seem completely healthy at birth, but after a few days it would begin to deteriorate, becoming more pale and weak, until eventually it died.

The most recent daughter of the unhappy couple had just been born and everyone did their utmost for the baby, trying to find out why she looked worse each day.

The news reached the neighboring village, where there lived a doctor who was an expert in the diseases of this world – and also in ailments that sometimes found no explanation other than the supernatural.

THE EXPERT DIAGNOSIS

The doctor examined the infant girl carefully. After ruling out any known illnesses, he reached the following conclusion:

"This child is the victim of a vampire witch, or *meiga*, as they are also called."

"Can you do anything for her?" asked the desperate father.

"First, I will perform certain magic tests to make sure that the infant's suffering really is the result of a vampire-witch attack."

After a divining rite using three river reeds, the doctor confirmed that he was certain a vampire witch was the cause of all the sad deaths in the family, as well as the present condition of the couple's new daughter.

THE REMEDY

"Is there a remedy, Doctor?" the mother asked.

"Let's hope so," the sage replied. "But before I do anything, I must ask you if you have ever sat up all night beside the baby."

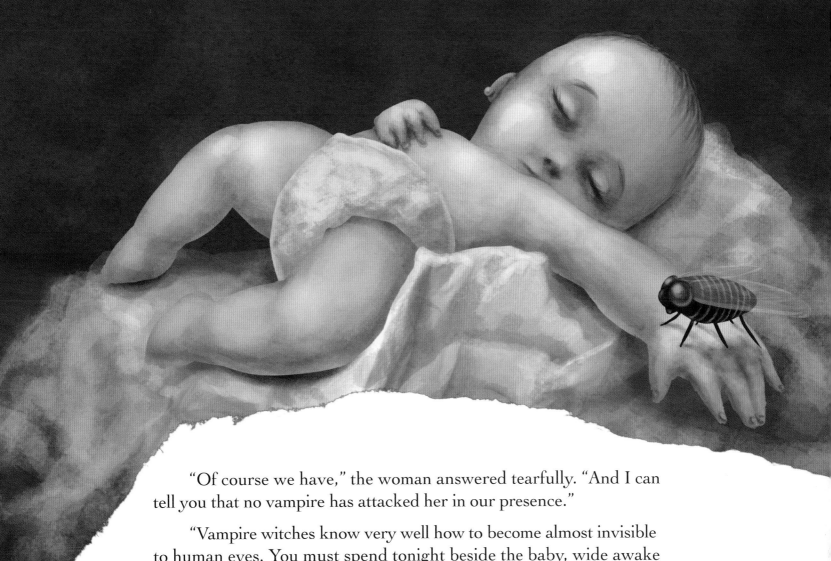

"Of course we have," the woman answered tearfully. "And I can tell you that no vampire has attacked her in our presence."

"Vampire witches know very well how to become almost invisible to human eyes. You must spend tonight beside the baby, wide awake the whole time, without taking your eyes off her. At some point, you will probably notice quite a large black fly, which will settle on the girl. When this happens, one of you must strike the insect with a hazelnut branch, while the other calls on St. Sylvester."

THE BLACK FLY

As the sun was setting, the parents entered their baby's room and, as usual, did not leave her.

Minutes after the living-room clock chimed midnight, they saw an insect flying toward the cradle. The baby was restless, but did not wake up. She uttered a faint groan just as the fly landed on one of her little hands. It was a monstrous black fly, the biggest they had ever seen. It rubbed its feet together, as if eagerly anticipating the idea of sucking sweet blood from the tiny girl.

The father got up and struck the revolting insect with the hazelnut branch, while the mother called upon St. Sylvester. The fly, completely and inexplicably, vanished.

A Death in the Village

In the morning, happy news spread quickly through the village. That night, a disagreeable and much disliked old woman, whom many suspected was a *meiga*, died suddenly and from no apparent cause. Everyone in the village, on hearing the doctor's explanation for the little girl's illness, had been suspicious of her. Now, they were absolutely convinced that the horrible old woman was none other than the vampire witch.

That very day the precious child began to show clear signs of recovery. For the first time since her birth the couple slept, confident that their baby was safe, and that they would watch her grow up strong and happy.

end

Mount Wawel Castle
polish legend

The Three Soldier Friends

In mid-winter 1915, during the sad times of the First World War, there was a large number of soldiers garrisoned in Cracow. Three of them were great friends, and, whenever they could, they enjoyed sitting around a small fire and telling each other stories of terror. For a little while, those stories helped them to forget the horrors of war. "There's nothing better than scary fantasy to distract us from real atrocities," one of them used to say.

One night, the soldier named Alexander decided to tell his friends the story of a vampire that, according to various legends, lived in nearby Mount Wawel Castle.

A Family Tragedy

"There was once the worst kind of vampire," Alexander began, "a horrendous beast that laid waste to the region for centuries until the legendary hero, Krakus, managed to kill it. To commemorate his great feat, the hero decided to build a castle on Mount Wawel, right where the vampire's lair had been."

"But that was too long ago to be interesting," his friend, Jaroslaw, complained. "That vampire's been dead so long, nobody cares about it anymore."

"You're wrong," Alexander replied. "The story of Krakus is just the beginning. According to legend, there was a family of nobles, the Bopiestz, who established themselves in the castle some two hundred years later."

"This is promising," Casimir, the third and youngest friend commented.

"For many years," Alexander continued, "the Bopiestz Family lived very happily. They often organized huge parties, and the castle was a joyous place."

"But some tragedy's going to occur," cut in Jaroslaw impatiently.

"Yes, yes, of course, and the tragedy took place on the wedding night of the family's only son, Lech. He married the German princess, Uswika. On their wedding night, a stranger knocked at the castle gate, asking for lodging. They happily gave him shelter, but next morning the family was horrified to find that Lech and his bride lay dead in their chamber, completely drained of blood. The newcomer had vanished, and the old vampire had returned."

A Rash Excursion

"What happened next?" asked Jaroslaw.

"The inhabitants of the castle fled, of course. Vermin filled the grain stores, the wine cellars flooded, and moss and cobwebs covered the entire building. No one has ever dared visit the sinister castle since!"

"Seriously? No one? Then we must go!"

"What are you saying?" interrupted Casimir, who was more frightened than the others by these legends of terror.

"We have a few days of leave coming up," Alexander remembered. "We could spend the night at the castle."

"Yes, let's invite some girls from the village and go up there to spend the night. We'll take some wine and food and have a great time," Jaroslaw decided.

For awhile Casimir tried to dissuade his two companions, but in the end he got tired of being a poor sport and agreed that the excursion would be fun, after all.

THE ILL-FATED NIGHT

When their time off finally came, the three friends went into the nearby village and managed to convince three girls they knew to accompany them on an excursion to the castle. The six young people spent a very enjoyable day together, and as night was falling, they reached Mount Wawel Castle.

To their great surprise, the castle truly was completely abandoned. Alexander had thought that the rumors of the sinister swamp, the moss and cobwebs, were nothing but rumors that circulated in the surrounding countryside.

As none of the young men were prepared to show signs of cowardice, they joked around for a little while and then decided to go in. They opened the heavy door to the main entrance and looked for a room with a fireplace, where they could sit in comfort and enjoy the cheese and wine they had brought.

After a while, the six had succeeded in forgetting their spooky surroundings and were having a great time, laughing, telling stories, and even singing.

But then they heard an unexpected noise. There was no room for doubt: someone was knocking at the door.

THE VISITOR

Alexander went to see who it was. He came back accompanied by a man whose appearance was simply hair-raising. He had a remarkably emaciated face and was extraordinarily pale. Such a strange face made his age impossible to guess, though his skin was wrinkled and his skull was completely bald. The tall, thin visitor looked like a skeleton in mourning. He gazed at each of the young people's faces in turn, with hate-filled, flashing eyes. Then his thin purple lips parted, revealing fangs that could have belonged to a wild animal. The girls screamed, and the lads placed themselves between them and the beast, in order to protect them.

From that moment on, chaos and panic ruled the room. That bloodthirsty creature launched an attack with all the fury he possessed, and soon it was clear there was no way of stopping him.

DAYS LATER

Days later the young soldiers had still not returned to barracks. Word spread that they had gone on an excursion to the castle. As a result, a patrol was sent to look for them. On arrival, the search party found the corpses of the three village girls and two of the lads. Only the youngest, Casimir, had survived, but he was hysterical and on the verge of madness.

Upon examination, it was discovered that the throats of the five bodies had been crushed and a large amount of blood had been drained. Casimir described the terrifying visitor and everything he could recall of the bloody struggle, but the doctors decided that the young man must have had too much drink along with his frightening experience, and that his story was unreliable at best.

However, those in the villages near the castle did not hesitate to believe the tale. They knew the tragic incident was due to the return of the most bloodthirsty and infamous vampire that had ever roamed the night as the living dead.

end

The Warriors of the Crypt

Danish Legend

THE VIKING TOMB

They say that very many years ago a powerful Swedish knight, who enjoyed exploring new places, visited a small village in Denmark with his troops. The men had been journeying for several days, and a picturesque village seemed the best place to rest and restore their strength.

On the first night, accompanied by several local villagers, they enjoyed a magnificent supper at the inn. The knight, who was always curious, began asking about many of the things he had seen during the day. What had most impressed him was a bronze tomb, carved with elegant animal figures, among them a dragon.

"That is the tomb of Assmeith and Asmund," the innkeeper explained. "It's a Viking tomb, and there's an interesting legend about it. Would you like to hear it?"

The knight and several of his men expressed their interest, so the innkeeper started to tell the story.

THE STORY OF ASSMEITH AND ASMUND

"There have never been two friends as greatly devoted to each other as Assmeith and Asmund. It is said that they knew each other from childhood, and when they were still barely adolescents, Assmeith saved Asmund from drowning.

"When they grew to adulthood, Assmeith and Asmund became companions in arms and felt so close that they swore a peculiar vow. They agreed that if one of them was mortally wounded and died before the other, the survivor would go into the tomb alongside his dead friend.

"You must know that the Vikings lived in Denmark until the eleventh century, engaging in countless bloody battles in an effort to conquer most of Western Europe. Well, in one of those skirmishes, Assmeith was killed, and Asmund did not hesitate to fulfill his promise.

"First he ordered a funeral mound to be built, as was the custom of that time. Then, before the large tomb was closed, he sat beside his dead companion and ordered all their possessions, including their weapons and horses, to be placed alongside them. Finally, the tomb was closed with the two friends, one living and one dead, inside."

THE SECRET TOMB

"Then what happened?" asked the knight, completely spellbound.

"No one knows," the innkeeper replied. "The tomb has been sealed ever since and the truth is that the villagers are terrified to approach it. What is certain is that Asmund is as dead as his companion, as over a century has passed since he decided to be buried alive."

"Tomorrow morning we must go and visit this tomb," the knight said. "Don't you agree that this story is fascinating?" he asked his companions.

At dawn, the group of Swedish soldiers set out for the burial mound. More than one had the same idea in mind: they had to open the tomb. Only then would they discover the secret it sheltered.

THE COMBAT

The knight and several of his men knelt together at Assmeith and Asmund's tomb.

"Do you hear something?" asked one of the men.

"That story we heard last night is undoubtedly putting suggestions in my head. I seem to hear the clashing of swords in battle. This is crazy!"

The others confessed that they thought they heard something similar. With no further hesitation, the men began to dig. When the tomb was completely open, the metallic ring of two swords striking each other was unmistakable. It was definitely the sound of combat.

"What should we do now? It's certain there are at least two warriors fighting it out down there," one of the soldiers said.

"Lower a rope, and I will climb down," the knight ordered.

THE WARRIOR'S RESCUE

The noble tied the cord around his waist and lowered himself into the deep, dark tomb. A few minutes later, the clashing of swords stopped, and everyone above began to worry.

Two soldiers were about to descend when the knight signaled them to pull him up. To everyone's surprise, he was not alone. An imposing Nordic warrior, dressed in ancient armor, accompanied him. He was very weak, clearly near death. But before accepting his fate, Asmund – for that's who it was – wanted to tell his story, as was the custom of his people. Engrossed, all the men listened.

ASMUND'S STORY

It didn't take long for Asmund to reach the part of the story that no one knew.

"After the tomb was closed and darkness surrounded me and my dead comrade, I can only guess that a demon entered Assmeith's body. Otherwise, I cannot explain why his corpse stood up and began to devour the horses.

"When he had finished with the poor animals, Assmeith, whose eyes were so intense they glowed in the dark, stared at me with terrifying cruelty. I would say he looked at me with hunger, and I knew he was about to hurl himself at me. I unsheathed my sword and became embroiled in a ferocious struggle with the corpse that has lasted for centuries – until your arrival, gentlemen.

"Only when the tomb was opened, did my opponent retreat, as if blinded by the sunlight. That is when I saw the hawthorn branch, a memento from my betrothed, with which I had been buried. Without a second thought, convinced that my faithful friend was now a ruthless vampire, I thrust the branch into his heart, killing him."

His story told, Asmund accepted death with his soul at peace. The Swedish soldiers buried him with all the honors a hero deserves. Then, according to tradition, they brought Assmeith's corpse outside, with the stake still in it, to burn. Afterward, the men scattered its ashes thus ensuring the vampire would never ever return.

end

Authors of the Vampire Stories

Name: Abraham Stoker
Born: November 8, 1847
In: Clontarf, Ireland
Died: April 20, 1912
In: London, England
Known as: Bram Stoker
Profession: Novelist
Literary genre: Gothic novels, Romanticism

Name: Joseph Thomas Sheridan Le Fanu
Born: August 28, 1814
In: Dublin, Ireland
Died: February 7, 1873
In: Dublin, Ireland
Known as: Sheridan Le Fanu
Profession: Writer, journalist
Literary genre: Gothic and terror novels, Romanticism

Name: John William Polidori
Born: September 7, 1795
In: London, England
Died: August 24, 1821
In: London, England
Known as: Polidori
Profession: Doctor and writer
Literary genre: Terror novels, Romanticism

Name: Alexandre Dumas
Born: July 24, 1802
In: Villers-Cotterêts, Aisne, France
Died: December 5, 1870
In: Puys, France
Known as: Alexandre Dumas, *Père*
Profession: Novelist
Literary genre: Terror novels, Romanticism, Customs and Manners

Name of the possible compiler:
Abu abb-Allah Muhammed el-Gahshigar
Lived in the ninth century
The story of Scheherazade, which serves as a framework for all the stories, seems to have been added during the fourteenth century.

Vampire's Honor is a story collected in *The Thousand and One Nights*. The *gul* (male vampires) and the *gola* (female vampires) reach this state by dying violently.

Name: Alexander Nikolayevich Afanasiev
Born: June 29, 1826
In: Boguchar, Russian Empire
Died: October 11, 1871
In: Moscow, Russian Empire
Known as: A.N. Afanasiev
Profession: Folklorist, writer, linguist
Literary genre: Terror and mystery novels, Romanticism

Name: Alexei Konstantinovich Tolstoy
Born: August 24, 1817
In: St. Petersburg, Russian Empire
Died: September 28, 1875
In: Krasny Rog, Russian Empire
Known as: A.K. Tolstoy
Profession: Poet, dramatist and writer
Literary genre: Terror and mystery novels, Romanticism

Name: Ernst Theodor Wilhelm Hoffmann
Born: November 12, 1776
In: Königsberg, Eastern Prussia
Died: June 25, 1822
In: Berlin, Prussia
Known as: E.T.A. Hoffmann
Profession: Writer, composer, music critic, draughtsman, jurist
Literary genre: Fantasy, Romanticism

Name: Félix Rubén García Sarmiento
Born: January 18, 1867
In: Metapa, today Ciudad Darío, Matagalpa, Nicaragua
Died: February 6, 1916
In: León, Nicaragua
Known as: Rubén Darío
Profession: Poet
Literary genre: Romanticism

Vampire Legends

Li-Yung and the Vampire
Ancient Chinese Legend

The Vampire Witch
Galician Legend

Mount Wawel Castle
Polish Legend

The Warriors of the Crypt
Danish Legend